MW01041379

Enjoy!

[signature]

Scarecrow Finds a Friend

Written by Blume J. Rifken

with Illustrations by Carl W. Wenzel

Whirlpool
Press

Lewiston, New York

Published by:
Whirlpool Press
698 Northridge Drive, Suite 214
Lewiston, New York 14092

Scarecrow Finds a Friend
Text by Blume J. Rifken
Illustrations by Carl W. Wenzel

Publisher's Cataloging-In-Publication Data
(Prepared by The Donohue Group, Inc.)

Rifken, Blume J.
  Scarecrow finds a friend / Blume J. Rifken ; illustrated by Carl W. Wenzel.
   p. : ill. ; cm.
  Summary: Tally is a good witch who is losing her power to fly. A scarecrow she has befriended comes up with a clever plan to save her flying power.
   ISBN-13: 978-0-9796948-0-6
   ISBN-10: 0-9796948-0-9
1. Scarecrows—Juvenile fiction. 2. Witches—Juvenile fiction. 3. Friendship—Juvenile fiction.
4. Gratitude—Juvenile fiction. 5. Scarecrows—Fiction. 6. Witches—Fiction. 7. Friendship—Fiction.
8. Gratitude—Fiction. I. Wenzel, Carl W. II. Title.
PZ7.R5454 Sca 2008
[Fic]   2007933237

Book and cover design by Christine Nolt, Cirrus Book Design, www.cirrusbookdesign.com
Art Direction by Penelope C. Paine, Santa Barbara, California
Edited by Gail M. Kearns, To Press and Beyond, www.topressandbeyond.com
A special thanks to Katheryne Gall

Printed in China

For Andrew and Nicholas

Scarecrow was the happiest he'd been in a long time. It was November and now he could rest. The crops he had protected so well from the pesky birds had all been picked.

From his post overlooking the farm, Scarecrow smelled something sweet and spicy coming from the farmhouse kitchen. "Yummy, apple pie and pumpkin bread," he thought. It was Thanksgiving time again and Scarecrow surely wished he could have a piece of that pie. Tired from all the work he'd done, he soon fell into a deep sleep.

Scarecrow dreamed about his adventures during the year. His favorite adventure happened only a month before, at Halloween. That's when Tally, a friendly witch, appeared out of nowhere, flying really low. It surprised Scarecrow so much that he almost teetered off his post. "Whoa! You nearly scared me out of my straw!" he exclaimed. "Who are you and what are you doing here?"

"I'm Tally and I'm here to grant you a Halloween wish," she said, her cape flapping wildly in the air.

For a long time, Scarecrow had been wishing that he could go trick-or-treating just like the farmer's children, Seth, Holly, and Sue. "Can you dress me as a ghost and can we go trick-or-treating together?" he asked.

"Yes," replied Tally. "I have the power to make any wish come true." She waved her arms, and a sheet as big as a cloud appeared. Then she whisked Scarecrow off of his wooden post and dressed him in the huge white bed sheet.

Looking very ghostly, Scarecrow hurried into town with Tally before it got too dark. They raced from house to house filling their bags with delicious treats.

Scarecrow will never ever forget his first bite of chocolate candy corn!

Scarecrow was jolted awake. Someone flying crookedly through the field had awakened him. "Tally! I was just dreaming about you." he exclaimed. "I'm so glad to see you!"

"Me too!" said Tally, out of breath and nearly crashing into Scarecrow's post. She was clearly having a problem flying.

11

"What's happening to you?" Scarecrow asked worriedly.

"A terrible thing—my flying powers are weakening! I need your help. I've been granting so many wishes that I can't seem to fly right anymore."

"How can that be?" asked Scarecrow.

"When I was very young my mother gave me a warning. She said I could lose the power to fly if I granted too many wishes. But she also told me there was a way to get my flying powers back. I never found out how though."

"Hmmm," Scarecrow thought aloud. "Maybe now it's your turn to be granted a wish."

"You think so?" Tally asked. "But who would grant ME a wish?"

Scarecrow knew they needed a clever idea. "Tomorrow is Thanksgiving," he said. "That means turkey, and a turkey has a wishbone. I think I have a plan that just might work...!"

The next day the smell of roasting turkey filled the air—all the way out to the field where Scarecrow and Tally were waking up.

"I need you to pull out a bunch of my straw," Scarecrow instructed Tally. Tally did just that and when she had finished, Scarecrow looked awful! Straw was hanging out everywhere, with most of it lying on the ground.

"What's next?" asked Tally.

"Now all we have to do is wait for dinner to be over," said Scarecrow, feeling a little weak. "Then the three children will come out to the field to play like they always do. When they see me like this, they'll want to take me inside to fix my stuffing. Then you follow them into the house and get the wishbone from the Thanksgiving turkey and bring it back here for us to wish on."

But waiting was too much for Tally. She became fearful. "What if your plan doesn't work?"

"Oh, Tally, please don't worry. My plan will work, I promise," reassured Scarecrow. "All you have to do is stay out of sight and get the wishbone. It'll be right there in the kitchen."

Late in the afternoon, Seth, Holly, and Sue dashed out of the house, all jabbering at once, as they headed toward the field.

Seth was first to notice Scarecrow's condition. "Look!" he yelled, "Scarecrow needs our help!" Seth and his two sisters ran up to Scarecrow and gently lifted him from his wooden post.

Carefully they carried him into the house with Tally following

right behind. She slipped into the hallway just before the door

slammed shut.

The children scrambled around the house looking for fresh straw. In a basket in the kitchen, they found some that had been left over from holiday decorating. Then they began replacing Scarecrow's stuffing.

Meanwhile, Tally was in the kitchen searching high and low for the wishbone. She looked on the countertops, by the sink, on the floor, and inside the refrigerator. She even went outside to look in the trash. No wishbone!

Tally was very disappointed and sad. She heard the children getting ready to take Scarecrow back to the field. She knew she had to leave and follow them. Scarecrow would be waiting for her.

Seth, Holly, and Sue reattached Scarecrow to his post. "Now Scarecrow looks plump and better than ever," said Seth. Then he and his sisters ran back to the farmhouse.

Scarecrow was delighted with how well he thought his plan had worked until Tally appeared all teary-eyed.

"There was no wishbone. I looked all over and it wasn't there. It looks like I'll never get my wish," she said.

"Oh, no," said Scarecrow, sadly. "What will we do now? We'll have to think of something else."

Just then a big wind blew across the farmer's field. It felt like a storm blowing in. Leaves were flying everywhere. Scarecrow's arm flapped so wildly in the air he thought he might lose it. Tally tried to help him but the wind was too strong. At that moment, the wishbone flew out of Scarecrow's sleeve.

Tally picked it up. Then she jumped up and down excitedly and Scarecrow would have too if he hadn't been attached to the post.

"How did that get in there?" Scarecrow wondered.

"It must have been in the straw from the kitchen, which the children used for your stuffing," said Tally. She looked at the wishbone. The straw had made it nice and dry. Now Tally could wish for her flying powers to return.

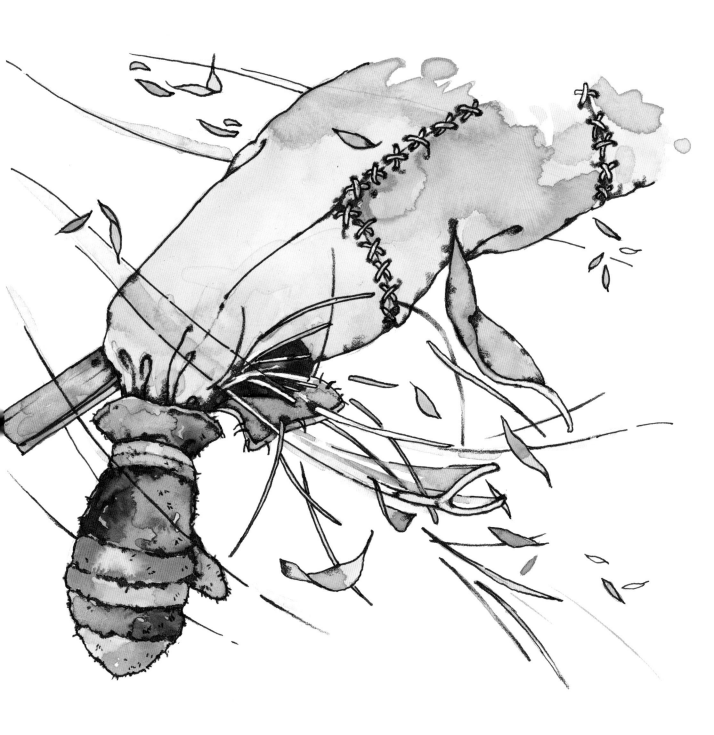

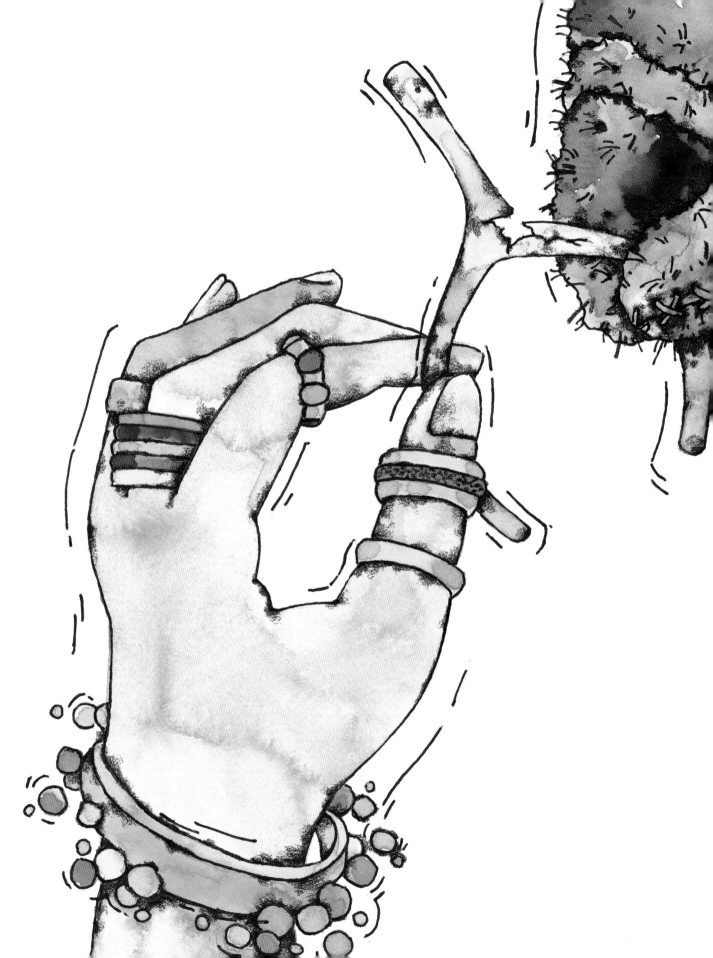

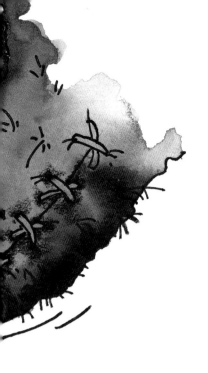

"Hold on," she said, giving Scarecrow one end of the wishbone while she held on to the other end. Tally and Scarecrow each made a wish as she yelled, "1-2-3 pull!" They pulled with all their might.

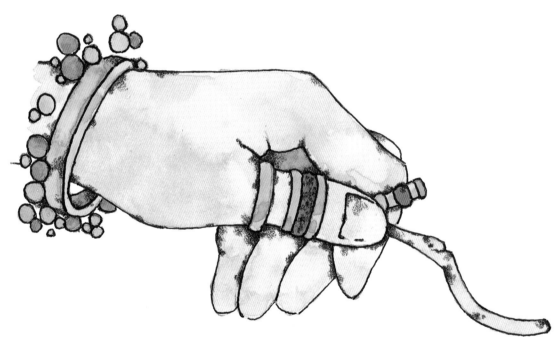

Crack! The wishbone split apart. Scarecrow and Tally looked down at the ends of the wishbone and saw that Tally's was the longest!

"Wow!" said Tally, "Your plan worked! It really worked!" She danced and flew around Scarecrow.

"I have something to tell you, Tally," said Scarecrow. "My wish was the very same as yours, so you couldn't lose. No matter who had the longest end, your wish would still come true."

"No wonder you promised that the plan would work. Thank you for helping me! You are a great friend!" exclaimed Tally.

"And so are you," said Scarecrow, happily.

Tally put her arms around Scarecrow
and hugged him tightly.

Then Scarecrow's friend flew away
with all the speed and power that she
had at Halloween, never to lose any of it
ever again.